"I DON'T LIKE CHOOSE YOUR OWN ADVENTURE® BOOKS. I *LOVE* THEM!" says Jessica Gordon, age 10. And now, kids between the ages of six and nine can choose their own adventure, too. Here's what kids have to say about the new Skylark Choose Your Own Adventure® books.

"These are my favorite books because you can pick whatever choice you want—and the story is all about you."
—**Katy Alson,** *age 8*

"I love finding out how my story will end."

—**Joss Williams,** *age 9*

"I like all the illustrations!"
—**Sarritri Brightfield,** *age 7*

"A six-year-old friend and I have lots of fun making the decisions together."
—**Peggy Marcus** *(adult)*

Bantam Skylark Books in the Choose Your Own
   Adventure® Series
Ask your bookseller for the books you have missed

GORGA, THE SPACE MONSTER

EDWARD PACKARD

ILLUSTRATED BY PAUL GRANGER

A BANTAM SKYLARK BOOK®
TORONTO • NEW YORK • LONDON • SYDNEY

RL 2, 007-009

GORGA, THE SPACE MONSTER

A Bantam Skylark Book / November 1982

CHOOSE YOUR OWN ADVENTURE® is a trademark of Bantam Books, Inc.

Original conception of Edward Packard

*Published simultaneously in hardcover and Skylark editions
November 1982*

Library of Congress Cataloging in Publication Data

Packard, Edward, 1931-
Gorga, the space monster.

(Choose your own adventure)
Summary: The reader is given choices to make which determine the
outcome of an adventure with a space monster who arrives in Cape Cod.
[1. Monsters—Fiction. 2. Literary recreations]
I. Granger, Paul, ill. II. Title. III. Series.
PZ7.P1245Go 1982   [E]   82-11539
ISBN 0-553-05031-1
ISBN 0-553-15161-4 (pbk.)

Published simultaneously in the United States and Canada

PRINTED IN THE UNITED STATES OF AMERICA

0 9 8 7 6 5 4 3 2

For Amy,
with appreciation

READ THIS FIRST!!!

Most books are about other people.

This book is about you!

What happens to you depends on what you decide to do.

Do not read this book from the first page through to the last page. Instead, start on page one and read until you come to your first choice. Then turn to the page shown and see what happens.

When you come to the end of a story, go back and start again. Every choice leads to a new adventure.

Are you ready to meet Gorga, the Space Monster? Then turn to page one . . . and good luck!

It's summertime, and you're visiting your grandpa and grandma at their house on Cape Cod. Every day you walk along the beach and dash in and out of the big ocean waves.

Late one afternoon, while you are walking over the sand dunes, you spot something that's round and looks sort of like a purple igloo. Igloos are *never* purple. And they're never on Cape Cod in the summertime! So you hurry to see what it really is.

As you get closer, the top part of the igloo lifts up and twists toward you. You can see three enormous green eyes looking right at you! It lets out a noise that sounds like "G-O-R-R-G-A."

You're not looking at an igloo. You're looking at a monster!

If you run back to tell your grandparents what you saw, turn to page 2.

If you stay where you are to see what happens next, turn to page 4.

2   "GORGA, GORGA!" you hear the monster roar, as you turn and start running back home.

You're glad to find Grandma waiting for you at the door. "We were worried about you," she says. "We just heard on the radio that a monster from outer space has landed right here on Cape Cod!"

"I *saw* it!" you cry, "out on the dunes!"

That night you can't stop talking about Gorga. Grandma tells you not to walk on the dunes or to go near the woods. "Monsters usually aren't friendly," she says.

The next morning you wonder whether to tell your friend Pete about Gorga, or to go to the dunes and see if there is any sign of the monster.

If you decide to visit Pete, turn to page 6.

If you decide to walk down to the dunes (even though Grandma told you not to), turn to page 9.

4   As you stand watching, Gorga stands up. He looks like a small hippopotamus. His mouth is half as big as his body.

Where could this monster have come from?

You watch as he eats a branch and then gobbles another and another! Suddenly he turns toward you. "G-O-R-GA, G-O-R-GA!" he bellows.

Maybe *Gorga* is his name!

"Hello, Gorga!" you call.

You see a piece of driftwood nearby. Maybe Gorga would like some dessert. You pick it up. It's about the size of a baseball bat. Suddenly Gorga starts coming right at you. His huge mouth is wide open!

Does he want to eat the log, or does he want to eat *you*?

If you try to protect yourself by hitting Gorga over the head with the log, turn to page 11.

If you just toss the log in front of Gorga, turn to page 13.

6   "Come on in," says Pete, when you reach his house.

"Wait till you hear what I saw yesterday!" you say.

"Wait till *you* see what's on T.V.!" he answers.

You follow Pete into the living room. A newsman is on the T.V. screen. His face is grim. *"The monster has been eating bushes and even small trees! It's already as big as an elephant, and it's growing bigger every hour!"*

"My gosh!" says Pete.

"Shhh!" you say, as the newsman goes on. *"The police have the monster surrounded. If no one can think of a way to stop it from eating so much and growing so fast, they may have to shoot it!"*

You're a little afraid of Gorga, but you would hate to see him get shot! Maybe you could get him to stop eating.

If you call the police and beg them not to shoot Gorga, turn to page 15.

If you decide to go right to the sand dunes, turn to page 18.

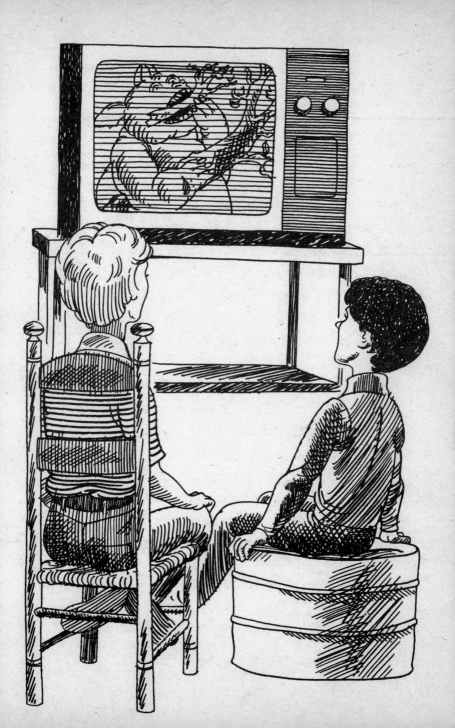

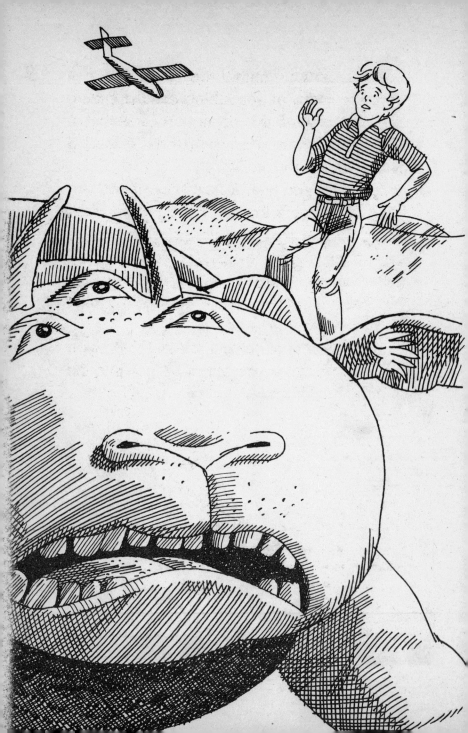

You follow the path through the dunes. A dog is barking at something on the beach. Looking toward the noise, you see that a large purple hump is rising from behind a dune. It's Gorga!

Just then you hear a noise above you. An airplane is flying low over the beach. Suddenly Gorga starts toward you. You jump out of the way as he passes you. Looking back, you see Gorga heading for the woods. He wasn't chasing *you*—he was running away from the airplane!

Now, instead of being afraid of Gorga, you feel sorry for him. You follow his trail into the woods.

Turn to page 40.

You take the driftwood log and try to bring it down as hard as you can right over Gorga's middle eye. But the monster is too fast. He closes his jaws around the log.

Gorga might not have meant to take such a big bite and eat you, too, but that's what he did!

The End

You toss Gorga the driftwood log. He opens his huge mouth and swallows it whole. You look for another piece of driftwood. Out of the corner of your eye you see Gorga waddling toward you, but he's so big and clumsy that you are able to keep him at a safe distance. Then you realize that he isn't chasing you, he's following you. Maybe he wants to be your friend!

What should you do?

If you run home as fast as you can to get away from Gorga, turn to page 2.

If you let Gorga follow you home, turn to page 21.

You hope you can get the police not to shoot Gorga. You pick up the phone, dial zero, and say, "Get me the police!" A minute later you reach the chief himself. You explain why you're calling.

"Look," he says. "The space monster has already eaten dozens of trees, eight telephone poles, and even part of a house. I can't believe some kid is going to stop him."

You keep arguing until the chief agrees to meet you at the scene. Within five minutes you are standing on the beach. Every policeman in the town is there. Gorga, the Space Monster, is only about fifty feet away, chewing on an old rowboat.

"Gorga!" you yell. "It's me! STOP!"

You are so close to Gorga that you can see your reflection in one of his big green eyes. Gorga just looks at you. Suddenly he drops the rowboat back onto the beach.

The police chief is amazed. "Hold fire, men!" he yells.

"Thanks, Gorga!" you call.

Go on to page 17.

The police chief throws an arm over your **17** shoulder. "I'm sure glad we didn't have to shoot Gorga. Now tell me, what do you think we should do with him?"

The End

18   You run down the path toward the dunes to see what's happening on the beach. Gorga is right in front of you, and he's much bigger than when you first met him. His huge purple mouth opens wide and keeps opening, wider and wider and wider. You turn and run for your life.

Fortunately, you are a pretty fast runner. That's why you're alive right now!

The End

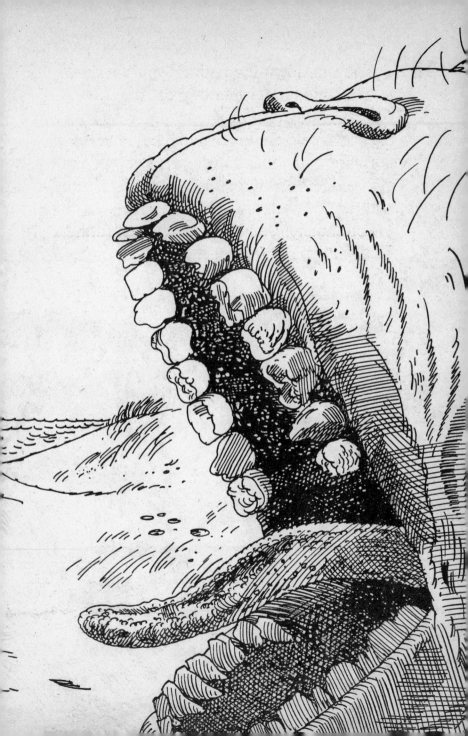

As you and Gorga walk home, people on the beach stare at Gorga. One of them yells, "Run for your life!" But you just keep walking. You feel sure that Gorga won't hurt you.

When you reach the house, Grandma and Grandpa are waiting at the door. "Quick! Come inside," yells Grandpa, "and let's hope that monster won't break the door!"

"I'm calling the police," says Grandma.

"Gorga won't hurt anyone," you say. "He eats only branches and driftwood!"

"So far," says Grandma.

"Can't Gorga stay with us?" you ask. "I'll make sure he doesn't do anything wrong."

Go on to page 22.

22   "I guess you can keep Gorga as long as he doesn't cause trouble," says Grandpa.

"And as long as he doesn't come in the house!" says Grandma.

There are some woods near the house with lots of sticks and branches that Gorga should find very tasty. You walk toward the woods and Gorga follows you—waddling along like a hippopotamus. He stops for a moment to eat an old stump in the backyard.

Gorga finds a thick grove of wild cherry trees growing near the dunes. He settles down and starts munching happily.

You feel great. Your new friend has a home and plenty of food, and you will be able to visit him as often as you want.

Should you keep Gorga in the backyard, where you can keep an eye on him, or in the woods, where he's less likely to get in trouble?

If you keep Gorga in the yard,
turn to page 25.

If you keep Gorga in the woods,
turn to page 26.

You pile some wood in the middle of the **25** yard for Gorga to eat. By the time you go to bed, he is sound asleep.

In the middle of the night you are awakened by a loud gnawing sound outside. You jump out of bed and run to the window. Gorga is chewing away at the wooden pillars that hold up the front porch.

CRUNCH! CRUNCH! Gorga must like the taste of those pillars. But if he keeps eating them, the whole house will come down!

You rush downstairs and out the door. You've got to do something fast!

If you scream in Gorga's ear to try to get him to stop, turn to page 29.

If you try to prod Gorga with a stick to get him to go away, turn to page 31.

26   You decide it would be safer to keep Gorga in the woods. He seems happy there, but each day he eats more and more, and each day he grows bigger and bigger. At first he eats only stumps and branches. But then he begins to gobble up whole trees. Soon he has grown almost as big as a *huge* hippopotamus!

One day when you come back from visiting Gorga, Grandpa comes out to meet you. "Gorga has eaten too many trees, and he's grown much too big," he says. "The police are coming to take him away."

You run into the woods, where you find Gorga chewing on an oak stump. "Gorga," you say, "if only you weren't so big—I could find a place for you to hide."

Gorga sits there looking at you like a big, bad puppy.

If you try to get Gorga to hide in the ocean, turn to page 32.

If you wait for the police to come, turn to page 37.

You walk up close to Gorga. "If you don't stop eating," you scream, "the police will shoot you!"

As you shout these words, Gorga turns and, with one swift bite, gobbles up a small tree. He has grown so fast that he looks like *two* hippopotamuses rolled into one.

Again he opens his gigantic mouth.

Suddenly you're sitting in a tree. But the tree is inside Gorga, the Space Monster.

The End

You take a long stick and poke Gorga very
hard.

Garuup! Gorga bellows like an angry elephant and lopes off into the woods.

At least you've saved the house!

The next morning you wake up early. You run outdoors and look around. There's no sign of Gorga—he hasn't come back. You're glad he's not still eating the porch, but you're worried about him.

*If you go looking for Gorga,
turn to page 40.*

*If you wait for your grandma and grandpa
to wake up, turn to page 34.*

32 You've got to save Gorga from the police.

"Hide in the ocean!" you cry, pointing toward the beach.

Gorga's mouth stretches wider. You shrink back, but then you realize that the monster is smiling.

Gorga charges over the dunes and down the beach. You follow close behind. When he reaches the water, he looks at you with all three eyes. Then he crouches down as if he would like you to climb up on his back.

That's just what you do! Gorga waddles **33** out into deep water. You sit on his back like the captain of a ship.

"*Let's go!*" you shout. Gorga paddles through the billowing sea. You feel as if you are sailing and flying at the same time!

The End

34   When Grandma and Grandpa wake up, you show them how Gorga almost ate the whole front porch.

"We'd better call a carpenter," says Grandma.

For the next few days you see no sign of Gorga, but you hear T.V. and radio reports about him. One film shows Gorga coming into someone's backyard and eating up a picnic table and two benches!

One morning you turn on the radio and hear this news report:

"The monster from outer space has gobbled up hundreds of trees. It was last seen on Dune Road—eating a beach house! The police are going to try to capture it. Meanwhile, everyone should get to a safe place."

You run to tell Grandma and Grandpa the news.

"We'd better stop talking and get out of here!" says Grandma. "This monster is dangerous!"

You all jump into the car, and Grandpa **35** drives off. You want to get to a safe place. On the other hand, you're curious to see what will happen when the police try to capture Gorga. After all, he's your pet—in a way.

If you say, "Let's drive along Dune Road and see what happens," turn to page 42.

If you say, "Let's get as far away as possible," turn to page 46.

"I think you'd better stay here, Gorga. **37** Once the police see what a good monster you are, things will be all right. . . ."

Gorga says nothing.

Soon the police come. Gorga is too big to fit into the police van, so they post guards to watch him. Hundreds of people gather to see what's going on.

It takes the government a long time to decide what to do about Gorga. Finally they turn the woods into a national park. They give Gorga only one truckload of driftwood to eat each day so he won't grow too large. Even so, he grows bigger than a hippopotamus, bigger than an elephant, and even bigger than the biggest whale.

Go on to page 39.

One day, Gorga waddles down the beach
to the sea and swims away.

As far as you know, he is living out there,
somewhere in the Atlantic Ocean, right now!

The End

It's easy to follow Gorga's trail through the woods because of all the branches and small trees he's eaten along the way.

When you reach the other side of the woods, you see Gorga ambling across a field, headed toward the railroad tracks.

Uh-oh . . . those railroad ties are made of wood! Sure enough, Gorga grabs one with his teeth and starts to pull. You hear the screeching of metal twisting and the popping of spikes as Gorga twists the railroad tie out from under the tracks.

Then, in the distance, you hear a railroad whistle—the morning train is heading for town. But Gorga is ripping up the tracks! You must do something fast!

If you decide to run toward the train and signal it to stop, turn to page 45.

If you decide to try to get help, turn to page 52.

42   "Let's drive along Dune Road, Grandpa. Maybe we can see what's going on."

"All right," he says, "if it's all right with Grandma."

"I don't think it's a very wise thing to do," says Grandma, "but I must admit I'm curious myself."

Grandpa turns the car down the street that leads to Dune Road. Unfortunately, Gorga, the Space Monster, has just turned down the same street.

The sky is suddenly blocked out by a great purple cloud. But it is not a cloud.

Purple is the color of the inside of Gorga's mouth!

The End

Maybe you can stop the train. You start to run down the tracks. Behind you, you can still hear Gorga ripping out railroad ties. The train is speeding around a curve and heading toward you.

"Stop! Stop!" you scream, your arms waving up and down.

The friendly engineer sees you—and waves back!

"No, *stop!*" you cry again, pointing up ahead.

Now the engineer *does* see Gorga. He slams on the brakes and blows the emergency whistle. The wheels of the train lock and go skidding down the track with a horrible screech and a shower of sparks.

Turn to page 48.

"Let's get as far away as possible," you say.

"Yes," says Grandma. "We can drive to the Lakeview Inn and stay there overnight."

When you reach the inn, you find everyone downstairs watching the news. Gorga, the Space Monster, is on the T.V. screen. Now he looks as big as a whale.

Then a newsman comes on the screen.

"The monster is still eating and still growing! The police may have to shoot it in the morning!"

You go to bed that night wondering what will happen to Gorga, the Space Monster. You dream that you are riding on Gorga's back while he flies high above the oceans and on up into the cool blackness of space.

Never have you had a dream that seemed so real! You and Gorga sail past the moon and past the comets and stars on a journey to his home in another galaxy. The ride makes you happy. And you know that Gorga is happy, too.

You wake up in the morning thinking about your dream. Then you go downstairs

and turn on the T.V. The news is surprising.
Gorga, the Space Monster, has disappeared.
No one can figure out where he went.
   But you know.

The End

48 The train stops only inches away from Gorga, who sits there glaring at the locomotive. The engineer gets down from the cab and walks to the front of the train.

"Get out of here!" he shouts.

"Gor-r-r-ga-a-a-a," Gorga answers, not moving an inch.

The angry passengers have started getting off the train and are walking to see what has happened.

"Look! It's a monster!" Everyone is pointing and shouting. Gorga sits very still.

One man walks up to Gorga and looks at him closely, and then he comes right over to you. He holds out his hand. "Buckam's my name—Henry Buckam. I own a circus. Is that *your* beast over there?"

"Not really," you say. "I just found him on the beach."

"How much do you want for him?" says Buckam. "I'll pay anything you want. I can make millions of dollars! A purple monster with three eyes!"

Go on to page 51.

Mr. Buckam is nearly jumping up and down. Gorga looks at him suspiciously with all three eyes.

"Well, maybe we can make a deal," you say, "if you'll promise to take good care of Gorga!"

"No need to worry," Mr. Buckam grins. "I'll hire *you* to take care of him."

Mr. Buckam calls to his circus crew. They get off the train and make a special cage for Gorga. Mr. Buckam then pays to have the railroad tracks fixed and hires you to take care of Gorga every summer.

You learn to feed Gorga the right amount of wood to keep him happy without making him grow any bigger. Everyone you know comes to see you at work in the circus. And you introduce them all to your friend Gorga, the Space Monster.

The End

52   You don't see how you can stop the train by yourself, so you head for the station house—as fast as you can run. You see a group of people standing by the tracks waiting for the train.

"The train is going to crash!" you shout.

The people look at you strangely. Suddenly there is a loud THUD back up the tracks—and then a grinding sound. You see a big crumpled shape near the tracks. It's Gorga! He must have been hit by the train! You run to get a better look. Meanwhile, Gorga rears up, looks around and takes off toward the beach. The train hasn't hurt him a bit!

You follow his trail and get to the beach just in time to see him waddling into the ocean. In a few minutes you lose sight of him completely.

It was quite a summer vacation—you'll never forget it. And from now on, whenever you go to the ocean, you'll look for your friend Gorga, the Space Monster. Maybe some day you'll see him again.

The End

ABOUT THE AUTHOR

Edward Packard, a graduate of Princeton University and Columbia Law School, practices law in New York City. He developed the unique storytelling approach used in the CHOOSE YOUR OWN ADVENTURE® series while thinking up stories for his three children.

ABOUT THE ILLUSTRATOR

Paul Granger is a prize-winning illustrator and painter.